MAR 2022

Praise for *Small Pleasures*

"Clare Chambers is that rare thing, a novelist of discreet hilarity, deep compassion and stiletto wit whose perspicacious account of suburban lives with their quiet desperation and unexpected passion makes her the twenty-first-century heir to Jane Austen, Barbara Pym and Elizabeth Taylor. *Small Pleasures* is both gripping and a huge delight. I loved what she did with the trope of the claim of a virgin birth, and how the hope of a miracle opens the door to love, kindness and hope in an arid existence. This is better than *Eleanor Oliphant Is Completely Fine* and deserves just as much acclaim."
— Amanda Craig, author of *The Lie of the Land*

"I adored *Small Pleasures*. It's engrossing and gripping: you want to race on and relish every sentence at the same time. I love the way Clare writes—her wry, subtle turns of phrase, the humor in the smallest of observations, the finely drawn characters. A wonderful book."
— Sabine Durrant, author of *Lie With Me*

"*Small Pleasures* is a gorgeous treat of a novel: the premise is fascinating, the characters are beautifully drawn and utterly compelling, the period setting masterfully and delicately evoked, and the plot is full of unexpected twists and turns. And oh, the finale broke my heart. I just couldn't put this novel down."
— Laura Barnett, author of *The Versions of Us*

"A delicious mystery and a touching exploration of loneliness and desire in cloying 1950s suburbia—a great read."
— Sally Magnusson, author of *The Sealwoman's Gift*

"*Small Pleasures* is the best sort of book: full of longing, regret and difficult emotions but leavened with so much warmth and humor it was a joy from start to finish."
— Francesca Jakobi, author of *Bitter*

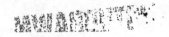

ALSO BY CLARE CHAMBERS